jF WARNER Gertrude
The disappearing
staircase mystery /
Warner, Gertrude Chandler,

WITHDRAWN

AUG 3

D0957598

*Th*

THE BOXCAR CHILDREN
SURPRISE ISLAND
THE YELLOW HOUSE MYSTERY
MYSTERY RANCH
MIKE'S MYSTERY
BLUE BAY MYSTERY
THE WOODSHED MYSTERY
THE LIGHTHOUSE MYSTERY
MOUNTAIN TOP MYSTERY
SCHOOLHOUSE MYSTERY
CABOOSE MYSTERY
HOUSEBOAT MYSTERY
SNOWBOUND MYSTERY
TREE HOUSE MYSTERY
BICYCLE MYSTERY
MYSTERY IN THE SAND
MYSTERY BEHIND THE WALL
BUS STATION MYSTERY
BENNY UNCOVERS A MYSTERY
THE HAUNTED CABIN MYSTERY
THE DESERTED LIBRARY MYSTERY
THE ANIMAL SHELTER MYSTERY
THE OLD MOTEL MYSTERY
THE MYSTERY OF THE HIDDEN PAINTING
THE AMUSEMENT PARK MYSTERY
THE MYSTERY OF THE MIXED-UP ZOO
THE CAMP-OUT MYSTERY
THE MYSTERY GIRL
THE MYSTERY CRUISE
THE DISAPPEARING FRIEND MYSTERY
THE MYSTERY OF THE SINGING GHOST
THE MYSTERY IN THE SNOW
THE PIZZA MYSTERY
THE MYSTERY HORSE
THE MYSTERY AT THE DOG SHOW
THE CASTLE MYSTERY
THE MYSTERY OF THE LOST VILLAGE
THE MYSTERY ON THE ICE
THE MYSTERY OF THE PURPLE POOL
THE GHOST SHIP MYSTERY
THE MYSTERY IN WASHINGTON, DC
THE CANOE TRIP MYSTERY

THE MYSTERY OF THE STOLEN MUSIC
THE MYSTERY IN THE BALL PARK
THE ____ SUNDAE MYSTERY
THE ____ HOT AIR BALLOON
____ ORE
____ YSTERY
____ OLEN BOXCAR
____ CAVE
____ ON THE TRAIN
____ MYSTERY AT THE FAIR
THE MYSTERY OF THE LOST MINE
THE GUIDE DOG MYSTERY
THE HURRICANE MYSTERY
THE PET SHOP MYSTERY
THE MYSTERY OF THE SECRET MESSAGE
THE FIREHOUSE MYSTERY
THE MYSTERY IN SAN FRANCISCO
THE NIAGARA FALLS MYSTERY
THE MYSTERY AT THE ALAMO
THE OUTER SPACE MYSTERY
THE SOCCER MYSTERY
THE MYSTERY IN THE OLD ATTIC
THE GROWLING BEAR MYSTERY
THE MYSTERY OF THE LAKE MONSTER
THE MYSTERY AT PEACOCK HALL
THE WINDY CITY MYSTERY
THE BLACK PEARL MYSTERY
THE CEREAL BOX MYSTERY
THE PANTHER MYSTERY
THE MYSTERY OF THE QUEEN'S JEWELS
THE STOLEN SWORD MYSTERY
THE BASKETBALL MYSTERY
THE MOVIE STAR MYSTERY
THE MYSTERY OF THE PIRATE'S MAP
THE GHOST TOWN MYSTERY
THE MYSTERY OF THE BLACK RAVEN
THE MYSTERY IN THE MALL

THE MYSTERY IN NEW YORK
THE GYMNASTICS MYSTERY
THE POISON FROG MYSTERY
THE MYSTERY OF THE EMPTY SAFE
THE HOME RUN MYSTERY
THE GREAT BICYCLE RACE MYSTERY
THE MYSTERY OF THE WILD PONIES
THE MYSTERY IN THE COMPUTER GAME
THE HONEYBEE MYSTERY
THE MYSTERY AT THE CROOKED HOUSE
THE HOCKEY MYSTERY
THE MYSTERY OF THE MIDNIGHT DOG
THE MYSTERY OF THE SCREECH OWL
THE SUMMER CAMP MYSTERY
THE COPYCAT MYSTERY
THE HAUNTED CLOCK TOWER MYSTERY
THE MYSTERY OF THE TIGER'S EYE
THE DISAPPEARING STAIRCASE MYSTERY
THE MYSTERY ON BLIZZARD MOUNTAIN
THE MYSTERY OF THE SPIDER'S CLUE
THE CANDY FACTORY MYSTERY
THE MYSTERY OF THE MUMMY'S CURSE
THE MYSTERY OF THE STAR RUBY
THE STUFFED BEAR MYSTERY
THE MYSTERY OF ALLIGATOR SWAMP
THE MYSTERY AT SKELETON POINT
THE TATTLETALE MYSTERY
THE COMIC BOOK MYSTERY
THE GREAT SHARK MYSTERY
THE ICE CREAM MYSTERY
THE MIDNIGHT MYSTERY
THE MYSTERY IN THE FORTUNE COOKIE
THE BLACK WIDOW SPIDER MYSTERY
THE RADIO MYSTERY
THE MYSTERY OF THE RUNAWAY GHOST
THE FINDERS KEEPERS MYSTERY
THE MYSTERY OF THE HAUNTED BOXCAR
THE CLUE IN THE CORN MAZE
THE GHOST OF THE CHATTERING BONES
THE SWORD OF THE SILVER KNIGHT
THE GAME STORE MYSTERY
THE MYSTERY OF THE ORPHAN TRAIN
THE VANISHING PASSENGER

THE GIANT YO-YO MYSTERY
THE CREATURE IN OGOPOGO LAKE
THE ROCK 'N' ROLL MYSTERY
THE SECRET OF THE MASK
THE SEATTLE PUZZLE
THE GHOST IN THE FIRST ROW
THE BOX THAT WATCH FOUND
A HORSE NAMED DRAGON
THE GREAT DETECTIVE RACE
THE GHOST AT THE DRIVE-IN MOVIE
THE MYSTERY OF THE TRAVELING TOMATOES
THE SPY GAME
THE DOG-GONE MYSTERY
THE VAMPIRE MYSTERY
SUPERSTAR WATCH
THE SPY IN THE BLEACHERS
THE AMAZING MYSTERY SHOW
THE PUMPKIN HEAD MYSTERY
THE CUPCAKE CAPER
THE CLUE IN THE RECYCLING BIN
MONKEY TROUBLE
THE ZOMBIE PROJECT
THE GREAT TURKEY HEIST
THE GARDEN THIEF
THE BOARDWALK MYSTERY
THE MYSTERY OF THE FALLEN TREASURE
THE RETURN OF THE GRAVEYARD GHOST
THE MYSTERY OF THE STOLEN SNOWBOARD
THE MYSTERY OF THE WILD WEST BANDIT
THE MYSTERY OF THE GRINNING GARGOYLE
THE MYSTERY OF THE SOCCER SNITCH
THE MYSTERY OF THE MISSING POP IDOL
THE MYSTERY OF THE STOLEN DINOSAUR BONES
THE MYSTERY AT THE CALGARY STAMPEDE
THE SLEEPY HOLLOW MYSTERY
THE LEGEND OF THE IRISH CASTLE
THE CELEBRITY CAT CAPER
HIDDEN IN THE HAUNTED SCHOOL
THE ELECTION DAY DILEMMA

# THE DISAPPEARING STAIRCASE MYSTERY

created by
GERTRUDE CHANDLER WARNER

*Illustrated by Hodges Soileau*

Albert Whitman & Company
Chicago, Illinois

Copyright © 2001 by Albert Whitman & Company

ISBN 978-0-8075-5491-3

All rights reserved. No part of this book may be reproduced or transmitted in
any form or by any means, electronic or mechanical, including photocopying,
recording, or by any information storage and retrieval system, without
permission in writing from the publisher.

THE BOXCAR CHILDREN® is a registered
trademark of Albert Whitman & Company.

Printed in the United States of America
10  9  8  7  6  5  4  LB  20  19  18  17  16

Illustrated by Hodges Soileau

For more information about Albert Whitman & Company,
visit our website at www.albertwhitman.com.

# Contents

# CHAPTER 1

# The Bugaboo House

The Alden house was jumping. Every few minutes, people on the front porch rang the doorbell. And every few minutes on the back porch, the family dog, Watch, whined to come in. The Alden children were in the kitchen baking cookies. Watch didn't want to miss any of the fun — or any of the crumbs, either!

Mrs. McGregor, the Aldens' housekeeper, handed Violet Alden two china plates. "I know you'll make a pretty pattern of cookies on these plates."

Ten-year-old Violet had careful hands. One by one she arranged the cookies into perfect circles. "I love when we have a lot of company," she told everyone in the Alden kitchen.

"And I love when we have a lot of cookies," Benny added. He was six. His job was to let Jessie know if the cookies were browning too fast. He and his five-year-old cousin, Soo Lee Alden, stared through the oven door window. They liked watching the lumps of cookie dough turn into round, crispy shapes.

The oldest children, fourteen-year-old Henry and twelve-year-old Jessie, watched the kitchen clock.

"Ten more minutes," Jessie announced. She was busy counting cups and saucers on a tray. "That's when Mabel said the meeting would start."

"Who's Mabel?" Soo Lee asked.

"Mabel Hart is Grandfather's good friend, Soo Lee," Jessie answered. "She runs a group called House and Hands. The helpers from her group fix up old houses for

people who need homes. We're going to be helpers, too," Jessie explained, peeking in the oven. "Looks like those cookies are done."

"At the meeting tonight, Mabel is going to introduce the volunteers to one another," Henry added. "We'll find out what jobs we'll be doing with the House and Hands group."

"Eating cookies is my job," Benny said when Jessie slid out the cookie sheet.

A few minutes later, the children joined Grandfather's guests in the living room. Nearly every chair was taken, even the creaky one next to the fireplace. The children carefully set the refreshments down on the coffee table. Then they found places to sit on the floor.

"Welcome to our home, everyone," Grandfather Alden began. "These are my grandchildren, Henry, Jessie, Violet, and Benny, and my grandniece, Soo Lee. Mabel Hart, our founder, has invited them to work on our first House and Hands project. They are hard workers. They fixed up a boxcar in the woods before I brought them here to live with me. You never saw such a cozy home as that boxcar. As for fixing things, they even fixed these cookies."

"Even though the cookies weren't broken," Benny added.

Everyone in the living room chuckled.

When the laughter died down, Mabel Hart stood up to speak. She was a tall woman with friendly blue eyes and a cloud of curly white hair. "As Mr. Alden said, our House and Hands group has a new fix-up project. This time around, we're fixing up a large house for twenty of our senior citizens to live in. The last owner left the estate to House and Hands. It used to be called the Bugbee House."

Everyone shifted and murmured.

"The Bugaboo House!" Benny whispered. "Wow!"

"Isn't the Bugaboo House haunted?" someone asked.

Mabel Hart smiled. "I knew that would come up. For years, there have been stories about the Bugbee House being haunted.

But our House and Hands engineers have checked out the property. They haven't found a single ghost! The place is just old and creaky. It just needs a lot of TLC."

Soo Lee raised her hand. "What's TLC?"

"Tender loving care," Mabel answered. "That's what we give to all our House and Hands projects. We have lots to do," she continued. "In a few days there will be an auction of everything in the Bugbee House. The money we make will help us buy building materials to fix up the property."

"I can't wait to get home to tell my wife and my grandkids about the auction," a man sitting nearby said.

"What's an auction?" Soo Lee asked.

"An auction is a big sale — almost like a show," Grandfather explained. "Somebody gets up in front and shows what's for sale item by item. People in the audience call out the price they want to pay. That's their bid. The person who bids the highest amount gets the item."

A man sitting nearby nodded. "There will be a lot of excitement over the Bugbee auction, I'm sure, Mr. Alden. Mr. Bugbee was quite a collector. I'm told he collected everything from jewelry and valuable books to old toys."

"Toys?" Benny and Soo Lee cried at the same time.

The man nodded. "Oh, yes. Mr. Bugbee and his wife collected a lot of fine old toys — trains, dollhouses, music boxes — all sorts of things. My grandkids will enjoy those. As for my wife and me, we like old books, antique jewelry, and such."

"Why would there be so many things in a house that nobody's lived in for years?" Violet asked.

"The story is that the Bugbees left town without taking a thing," explained Grandfather. "They sold the entire house and everything in it to another owner. He lived overseas and never moved in. Finally he donated the Bugbee House to the House and Hands group to fix up."

"Now, now, I'm sure they didn't leave *everything* in the house," said an older woman sitting nearby with her husband.

She turned to Mr. Alden. "I'm Louella Gardiner, and this is my husband, George. Anyway, everyone will discover what was left soon enough, won't they?"

"I suppose," Grandfather said. "I think Mabel has a few more announcements. Let's hear what she has to say."

Louella Gardiner turned back to talk with her husband, but her question made the children curious. Just what was there to discover at the Bugbee House?

Mabel Hart tapped her pen against her teacup to get everyone's attention again. "Before refreshments, I'd like to introduce our project leaders to the other volunteers," she announced. "Please meet Nan Lodge."

Everyone looked around the room.

"Nan!" Mabel repeated. "Stand up, please."

Finally a young woman with reddish-brown hair looked up from the notebook she was writing in. "Were you calling me? Sorry, Mabel. I was just going over my notes." She stood up and smiled nervously at the volunteers. Then she quickly sat down again and went back to her scribbling.

Mabel looked around the room. "Brian Carpenter is another one of our leaders. Brian, please give a wave so everyone can see who you are. House and Hands is delighted to have Brian. He's a construction worker who will supervise the building jobs."

Brian waved but didn't smile. He looked as if he belonged in a workshop with a power saw, not in a wing chair having tea and cookies. Like Nan Lodge, he seemed to be in his early thirties. He wore work boots, jeans, and a work vest filled with tools.

Mabel looked around the room. She picked out the Gardiners, who stood up. "Louella and George Gardiner have already begun the cleanup of the Bugbee estate. They're getting everything ready for the auction in a few days. They have worked on several fine old estates before," Mabel told everyone.

Mr. Alden stood up, too. "Please enjoy yourselves and have some refreshments. And do let the leaders know what your special talents and skills are. They will direct each person to the best job."

"Mine is making cookies and eating them," Benny told Grandfather. "I'm good at that job."

Jessie went over to Louella Gardiner, who was pouring herself some tea. "May we help you with the auction?" Jessie asked. "Our family has organized yard sales before. Henry and I are strong. Violet is good at arranging things. Benny and Soo Lee can fetch things."

"Children handling antiques? I'm afraid that wouldn't do at all," Louella said in a low, firm voice. "Mr. Gardiner and I have run many estate sales. I can assure you we don't use children to handle valuables. You may want to work with Nan Lodge or Brian Carpenter instead. I'm afraid we simply cannot have children underfoot." She walked away.

Henry tried to cheer up the other children. They were surprised that Louella had been so cross with them. "There's plenty to do besides working on the auction. Let's go see if Brian or Nan could use some Alden elbow grease."

Soo Lee and Benny checked their elbows.

"My elbows aren't greasy, Henry," Soo Lee said.

Henry picked up Soo Lee. He gave her a twirl until she giggled. "Elbow grease just means hard work, Soo Lee."

Brian Carpenter and Nan Lodge were looking over some papers when the Aldens came over.

"I'm in charge of repairs," Brian told Nan in a sharp voice. "I can't have volunteers running all over the house before the major repairs are done. I would suggest that you keep your workers busy with outside work until my crew finishes the heavy work on the upper floors. Then your volunteers can get on with the painting and such."

The Aldens stepped forward just as Nan stomped away.

"If you need help, Henry and I are pretty good at repairing things," Jessie told Brian. "You can check our boxcar in the backyard to see how we fixed it up."

Brian stared at Jessie before answering. "I'll let you know. This isn't a playhouse like your boxcar. It's a real house. I need a grown-up crew for now."

The children looked at one another, then walked away.

"Gee," Henry said. "The Gardiners don't want us to help out at the auction. Now Brian only wants grown-ups for his group. That leaves Nan Lodge."

The Aldens tracked down Nan in Grandfather's den. She was looking through some of his old books about Greenfield. She didn't hear the children enter.

"Sorry," Jessie said when Nan seemed startled to see the Aldens. "Can we help you find something?"

Nan put down the book she had been reading. "I was checking for some information Mabel needed. But I didn't find it. I'm going to get some tea." With that, Nan suddenly got up and returned to the living room.

"Let's wait to talk with the leaders when they're not so busy," Jessie suggested after

Nan left. "I wonder why Nan was looking through Grandfather's old books."

They went out to the living room, too. Everyone seemed to be buzzing with stories about the Bugbee family.

"Well, my uncle told me Mr. Bugbee and his family left Greenfield in disgrace. Something to do with unpaid taxes or some such thing," a volunteer said.

"What are taxes?" Benny whispered to Henry.

"It's money that people pay to the government," Henry answered. "Money that helps run the town of Greenfield and lots of other things."

"Oh!" Benny whispered. "That's important."

"Can you imagine just leaving your whole house and everything in it?" the volunteer went on. "The Bugbees must have been in some kind of big trouble."

The Aldens noticed how upset Brian and Nan looked when they heard this. Nan's face had turned white. Brian's was nearly as red as his flannel shirt. Both of them stared at the volunteer, who kept right on talking about the Bugbees.

Just in time, Grandfather joined the group. "No one really knows why the Bugbees left Greenfield. They were private people. I know they ran into difficulties and had to leave their home. That could happen to anyone."

The Alden children looked at one another without saying anything. They had left their own home after their parents died. Yes, leaving home could happen to anyone.

CHAPTER 2

## *Gloomy Rooms*

"I never saw this rusty old gate open before," Henry said when the Aldens arrived at the Bugbee estate a few days later.

The children stared up at the gate. They had passed it often, but it had always been locked before. Now it was open. The two stone lions on each side of the gate almost seemed to be guarding the entrance to the estate.

Violet shivered. "I wish it wasn't such a gloomy day. It will be too dark and wet for camping out."

Jessie motioned for everyone to follow her. "Don't worry, Violet. I stuffed our sleeping bags into big plastic bags so they'll be warm and dry. Besides, we're not camping in tents like some of the other volunteers."

"That's right," Grandfather agreed. "You'll be staying in a playhouse that Mr. Bugbee built for his children. Mabel said there's plenty of room for all of you."

"I made sure to pack our camp lantern, too," Henry said. "Did you bring your flashlight, Violet?"

"It's in my backpack," Violet answered. "Oooh, something just brushed my cheek!"

"Sorry, Violet," Henry said. "I let that branch swing back too fast. Here, I'll hold it for you."

All the bushes and trees on the Bugbee property were heavy and wet from the rain that had just ended. The branches kept brushing against the Aldens every which way.

Grandfather took out the small notebook he always carried everywhere. "I'll have to come back with my gardening tools to cut back these shrubs and vines. Why, you can hardly see any of the buildings on the property. Even the main house is half hidden by overgrown trees."

The Aldens stared at the old mansion. The tall pillars holding up the porch leaned in every direction. Many windows were cracked. Shutters dangled. Paint was peeling.

Just then, the Aldens jumped back when a figure suddenly appeared out of the bushes.

"Hello, Mr. Alden," Nan Lodge said. "I saw you come up the driveway with your grandchildren. Mabel asked me to bring them to the playhouse to drop off their things. Mabel's waiting for you in the main house, Mr. Alden."

After Grandfather left, Nan rushed the children around the property. She pointed out the broken-down greenhouse, the old stable, a garage, some old sheds, and a wonderful small building about half the size of the Aldens' boxcar.

"It's a playhouse!" Soo Lee said.

When the children looked inside, they were surprised to see a large person inside the child-sized building.

"Oh, hi, Brian," Henry said when he looked in the doorway. "We didn't expect to find anyone here."

Brian stood up from the small children's table and chair in the corner. He seemed startled to see Nan and the Aldens. "And I didn't expect to see you here, Nan. I needed to get away from all the bustle in the main house. The playhouse seemed as good a place as any."

"Mabel is going to let the Aldens camp out in here this week while they work on the house," Nan explained.

"What?" Brian said. "This place is falling apart. It hasn't been used for decades."

"How would you know that, Brian?" Nan asked. "You told me you didn't know anything about the Bugbee House."

Brian didn't answer right away. "Well," he said finally. "Anyone can tell by looking that there haven't been any kids in this playhouse for quite a while."

"That's about to change." Nan turned to the Aldens. "Mabel left that box of cleaning things for you in the corner. Maybe later in the week you can paint in here, too. I'll come back for you in a while. You're going back to the main house, too, right, Brian?" Nan asked.

"Right," Brian answered. He brushed past Nan and the Aldens without another word.

Nan sighed, then headed to the main house as well.

The Aldens didn't waste any time getting to work.

"Let's leave our bags on the porch until we sweep and dust," Jessie said. "Benny, you go fill that bucket from the garden hose. After we sweep, we'll wash down the floors."

While the younger children were gone, Henry found a hammer and began banging. "There are a lot of bent nails sticking out. I don't want us to snag ourselves."

Jessie handed Violet a sheet of sandpaper from the cleanup box. "Let's sand down the slivers and rough spots to get everything ready for a paint job."

Benny was groaning as he carried in the heavy water bucket filled to the brim.

Jessie laughed. "You didn't need to fill it quite so much. Let's pour some water into that smaller bucket to clean the woodwork and use the big bucket for the floor."

The Aldens spent the next hour scrubbing everything that could be scrubbed. By the time Nan returned, the playhouse gleamed. The children had lined up their sleeping bags on the floor. Their jackets and bags hung on a row of nails. Violet had even gathered a bunch of wildflowers and stuck them in an old milk bottle.

But Nan didn't seem to notice anything different. "Mabel needs you up at the house," was all she said to the Aldens after they'd done so much work. "Let's go."

"Wow," Benny said as they walked along. "Now we'll finally get to see the inside of the Bugaboo House."

"Don't call it that!" Nan said. She guided the Aldens up the stairs to the fancy porch.

"The Bugbees were a fine Greenfield family. They weren't spooky at all."

The children could hardly keep up with Nan when they entered the old mansion. She rushed them around from room to room on the first floor. Several volunteers were already up on ladders scraping old paint. Others were down on their knees hammering down loose floorboards or replacing them altogether. Everywhere the Aldens looked, people were busy.

One of the volunteers called out to the children, "Hey, Aldens! Mabel said to meet her in the kitchen."

Nan turned around. She pointed to a long hallway. "The kitchen is off that hall. Go ahead without me."

After Nan went off, Brian Carpenter appeared, looking for her. "Every time I turn around, Nan's off someplace. She didn't go upstairs, did she? Well, never mind. Go check in with Mabel and get out of all this hubbub in here."

The children went off. At the end of the

hallway, they found themselves facing a wall, not the kitchen.

"Nan never did say which door led to the kitchen," Jessie said. "Maybe she meant the hallway off this one."

The children retraced their steps partway, then headed down another hall. They found themselves in a separate wing of the house, which was empty and silent.

"This house seems so sad," Violet said. She opened a closet door. Three empty hangers hung on a rod. Lying on the floor was a broken umbrella someone had left behind.

"After we fix it up, this house won't seem so deserted anymore," Jessie said. "Benny, why don't you and Soo Lee run ahead. Check those doors off the hallway."

Benny liked nothing better than exploring new places. "Come on, Soo Lee." He leaned on the first door they passed. "It's locked."

Soo Lee tried a different door. "This one isn't locked. Look, there's another little hallway. Maybe that's the one that goes to the kitchen."

"Follow us," Benny yelled back to the other children.

The door closed behind Benny and Soo Lee. Except for a tiny crack of light coming from under the door, the space was completely dark.

Benny felt something hit his cheek. "What was that?" He reached up. "Whew! It's a string to turn on the light."

Even with a light on, Soo Lee stayed close to Benny.

The two children walked down the short passageway.

Benny discovered another door. "This one's locked, too," he said. "Hey, do you hear voices?" He tilted his head to hear better. "I can't tell who it is."

"Can we go back?" Soo Lee asked.

"I guess it was just some people talking in another room," Benny said.

Soo Lee and Benny walked back to where they had started. Benny tried to open the door, but the knob refused to turn.

"Are you two still in there?" Henry asked from the other side.

"We're here," Benny called out.

"The door must have locked by itself when you shut it," Henry said. "I'll try to find a key."

Benny felt a little braver now that his brother and sisters stood on the other side of the door. "We're going to try the next door down again. Maybe it's just stuck.

"When I push, you push me, okay, Soo Lee?" Benny said when he leaned against the door. "One, two, three, push!"

The door opened! Soo Lee and Benny found themselves just down the hall from the other children.

"Hey! Over here!" Benny called out.

Henry came over. "Good thing you found a way out. Mabel said she has no idea where the keys to all the doors are. She lent them to the Gardiners, but no one knows where they went. Oh, good. Here's Nan."

The children explained to Nan how Benny and Soo Lee had found another passageway.

"Did you get inside any rooms? Or find anything?" Nan asked. "Books, papers, anything unusual? I wish I had time to look around, but Mabel sent me to the hardware store."

"The Bugaboo House sure is a mixed-up place," Benny said. "All we found were doors and more doors."

"One of the engineers said there are over sixty doors in the house and different passages and levels," Nan told the Aldens. "Yesterday I opened one door, and behind it was just a wall."

"Wow!" said Benny.

"Yes, well, there's no time to explore now," said Nan. "It's time for the auction. The Gardiners have spent the last few days getting it organized, so let's go."

# CHAPTER 3

# Going, Going, Gone!

All of Greenfield seemed to be jammed into the Bugbees' old stable for the House and Hands auction. The Alden children strolled through the excited crowd. Unlike the grown-ups, they passed right by the displays of old furniture, mirrors, paintings, tools, dishes, and lamps.

"There are the toys!" Soo Lee cried, running ahead.

Off in a corner, the children spied a bookcase and a table with old toys displayed.

Benny and Soo Lee were excited. The older children looked at one another, puzzled.

"Somehow I thought there would be lots more toys," Henry whispered to Jessie and Violet. "I heard a lot of people saying the Bugbees had a huge toy collection."

"I see what you mean," Jessie agreed. "Still, Benny and Soo Lee seem happy with what's here."

Jessie joined Soo Lee. She was crooning over some old dolls, several of them with china heads. But the one Soo Lee fell in love with was a small stuffed doll made of faded cloth.

Over on the table was a collection of train cars and metal trucks, including a horse-drawn fire truck, a milk wagon, and even a toy ice wagon.

"Look," Benny said when he spotted a small train set. "This locomotive looks just like a real one."

Violet wandered over to a bookcase, where several toy music boxes were lined up on the shelves. "I like these," Violet said.

One of them had a dancing bear that spun around when the box was wound up. "Listen. It plays 'The Teddy Bears' Picnic.' Do you think I could bid on this?"

At that moment, Brian came over. "No one is supposed to touch these toys," he informed the Aldens. "George will show the audience how they work — that train set, this music box. Just leave it there."

"Brian!" a volunteer yelled from the doorway. "We need you to sign for some materials that just arrived."

Brian looked at the Aldens and sighed. "See you later. I never get a free minute around here."

"We'd better get to our seats," Henry told the other children when the Gardiners seemed about to begin the auction. "Grandfather saved us places in the third row."

George Gardiner stood in front of the crowd. He explained how the auction worked. Then he had one of the volunteers bring up an old painting to get the bidding started.

The Aldens followed the bidding care-

fully, though it moved very quickly. George put up one item after another for people to bid on — everything from vases to eggbeaters. As soon as an item was purchased, it was whisked away to a storage room in front of the stable.

The Alden children waited and waited, until finally it was time to auction the toys. One by one, the Gardiners held up each toy for the bidders.

"Here we have a small antique train set," George Gardiner announced finally. "Who will start the bidding?"

Benny jumped from his seat and waved his hand. "Fifty cents!" he shouted.

The whole crowd laughed. The set was definitely worth more than fifty cents.

"Never mind, Benny," Grandfather whispered. "I'll add a bit to your birthday money. You can go up to twenty-six dollars."

In no time, the Aldens were on the edge of their seats. George Gardiner raised his auction hammer for the final bid. "Twenty-five dollars. Going once, going twice . . ."

Benny stood up and shouted out, "Twenty-six!"

"Twenty-six dollars," George said to the crowd. "Going once, going twice . . ." He banged down the auction hammer. "Sold to the boy in the third row."

"That's me!" Benny said happily. "I won the train." He couldn't wait to see what the next item for sale would be. "There's the music box Violet wanted," he said.

George Gardiner wound up the dancing bear music box. The crowd quieted down to hear the pretty tinkling sound of "The Teddy Bears' Picnic."

"Who will start the bidding on this fine old music box?" George asked the crowd.

Violet could hardly sit still.

Grandfather leaned down to tell her something. "It's a good idea to wait for someone else to get the bidding started," he advised. "That way you're not running up the price too fast. Plus you get to see who else is bidding."

"Thank you, Grandfather," Violet whispered. She clasped her hands on her lap. "I'm so nervous."

A child in the front row called out a bid: "Three dollars."

Violet held her hands even tighter. "Should I bid now, Grandfather?"

"Not just yet."

"Three-fifty," a grown-up's voice said down the Aldens' row.

Pretty soon three more bidders called out bids for the music box. The bids went all the way up to seven dollars and fifty cents.

Violet still sat there patiently.

When no other bidders spoke up, George Gardiner called out, "I have seven dollars and fifty cents. Do I hear eight?" He waited, but no one said a thing.

"Going once," George began, "going twice . . ."

Grandfather gently poked Violet's elbow. "Now."

"Eight dollars!" Violet called out, loud and clear.

George nodded at Violet. "We have a

new bidder in the third row at eight dollars. Do I hear eight-fifty?"

"Eight-fifty!" said the girl who had started the bidding. Soon she and Violet bid against each other all the way up to ten dollars and fifty cents. They were the only two bidders left.

"I have eleven dollars from the dark-haired girl in the third row," George called out after Violet's last bid. "Going once, going twice . . ." He raised his auction hammer in the air then banged it down on the table.

"Twelve dollars!" a man's voice in back yelled out.

The Aldens turned around. The man's voice belonged to Brian Carpenter.

"Too late, Brian. I already brought the hammer down. That's the rule," George yelled back. "Violet Alden is the high bidder for the music box. Sold for eleven dollars!"

After Brian heard that, he turned and left the stable.

Violet bit her lip. "Oh, dear. I hope Brian

isn't too upset, Grandfather. I'm glad I won the box. I just wish he didn't want it, too."

"Not to worry," Grandfather told Violet. "That's how auctions are. It's a contest. I wonder why a big fellow like that wants a child's music box."

The Aldens went back to enjoying the auction. At the end of it, they each had won something they wanted.

"I'd been looking for another sturdy rake for a long time," Grandfather said as he and the children went to pay for their items. "Now I have one."

Soo Lee tugged on Jessie's arm. "Did I win my dolly?"

Jessie smiled down. "You sure did, Soo Lee. And I won a beautiful antique photo album that I can put pictures in. Let's go out to the storage area where we have to pay. Then you can pick up your doll."

Henry was pleased with his purchase, too. "Now I have a penknife to carve things with."

"I'm glad I won the dancing bear music box," Violet said. "That was close. I just hope Brian doesn't mind too much that I won it instead of him."

The Aldens strolled out to the storage area at the front of the stable. All the auction items people had bid on had stickers showing the final bid prices. The Gardiners seated themselves behind a table where the successful bidders lined up to pay.

"But it can't be the end of the auction," the Aldens heard a man say to Louella Gardiner. "I drove all the way from Maplewood to bid on Mr. Bugbee's collection of rare books. Why weren't they in the sale?"

"All you had for sale was fake jewelry," someone else complained. "My great-aunt told me Mrs. Bugbee had inherited some valuable jewels from her family. But this was just junk."

Several other people in the crowd murmured that the auction wasn't what they had expected.

The Gardiners waited for everyone to calm down.

Finally George spoke up loudly. "We put up everything that was left in the Bugbee

House. You'll recall that the house was sold to another owner. Anything could have happened to the Bugbees' collection. We only had a few days to get everything organized. We did our best. We've raised a great deal of money for the House and Hands group today."

After the crowd scattered, the Aldens paid for their items. Some of the fun of the auction was gone.

"At least I got my train set," Benny said.

"Louella," Violet asked. "Did you see the music box I bid on? I came to pay for it."

"Which music box?" Louella asked sharply. "There were several in the sale. I can't be expected to keep track of everything. Look where the toys are."

Violet checked the shelves. There wasn't a single music box on it. She swallowed hard. The dancing bear box was nowhere to be seen.

"Maybe somebody stole it," Benny said. Now that the auction was over, he was ready for more excitement.

"Nonsense!" George Gardiner told

Benny. "That box was barely worth what your sister bid on it. Thousands of those boxes were made years ago."

"It was worth more than money to me," Violet whispered, but the Gardiners didn't hear her. "I love the tune it played."

Soo Lee held out her new toy. "You can play with my doll, Violet."

"We'll keep an eye out for that box," Henry told Violet after he and the other children left the stable.

Violet looked back. Maybe someone would come running out with her music box after all. But the auction was over. Mr. Gardiner was pulling the doors closed. He and Louella were inside. There was no chance now that they would come out with Violet's music box.

"I think there's something strange about those two," Jessie said. "You'd think they would be interested in finding out more about the Bugbee collections from people who grew up here. They didn't even ask any questions."

"Maybe we should look around and see if

there's anything in the house that should have been in the auction," Henry said.

"And maybe we'll find Violet's music box, too, in case somebody stole it," Benny said, still hoping for an adventure.

"Well, let's look around when we're working in the big house," Jessie suggested. "We always find things when we're doing jobs."

# CHAPTER 4

## *Footsteps Overhead*

The next morning Jessie woke up with cold feet. She was used to Watch sleeping at the end of her bed and warming her feet. Only now Watch was at home while Jessie was in her sleeping bag in the Bugbee playhouse.

Soon everyone else's eyes were opening, too. It took a few minutes for the children to figure out where they were.

"It's so cozy in here now," Violet told Jessie as she stretched her arms out of her sleeping bag. "I like the way we fixed up this playhouse with the little table and our camp lamp. Maybe tonight Soo Lee can stay here, too."

The playhouse soon filled with sounds of sleeping bag zippers being unzipped and clothes being zipped.

"Brrr," Henry said. "It's always hard to get out of my sleeping bag. Let's hurry to the main house. Brian told Nan that they got the furnace working yesterday."

"I hope they got the hot chocolate working, too," Benny added.

The Aldens got dressed and hurried from the playhouse to the main house. It was cold and damp outside.

When they arrived, the kitchen table was piled high with good things to eat and drink for breakfast.

"Help yourselves to whatever you want," Mabel told the volunteers. "Don't be shy."

"We won't be," Benny said when he came to the table. "Yum, these look just like Mrs. McGregor's corn muffins."

"Those *are* Mrs. McGregor's muffins," Grandfather said with a laugh. "I brought them with me along with Soo Lee this morning. Mrs. McGregor and Watch miss you."

"Finish up, everyone," Mabel called out. "You'll find our job assignments on the work list." She turned to the Alden children. "I have a special job for all of you."

"What is it?" Benny and Soo Lee asked.

"I saw what a tidy job you did in the playhouse. Now I need helpers on the top floor of the nursery wing," Mabel said. "There are odds and ends to clear out before the electricians get to work. The third-floor nursery rooms are small. You children are just the right size for the job."

Soo Lee stood on her tiptoes. "But I'm big. My mommy said so."

Mabel smiled. "Yes, you are just the kind of big girl I need as a helper. Here are some cleaning supplies and a vacuum cleaner. Now off you go."

The Aldens were just gathering up everything when Nan came over.

"Did I hear you say the Aldens are to

clean out the nursery wing?" Nan asked Mabel.

Mabel nodded.

Nan's mouth tightened into a frown. "But, but I heard the Gardiners say they need help outside."

"Fine," Mabel said. "The children will help them after the nursery rooms are cleaned. See you later, Aldens."

The children climbed several sets of creaky, winding stairs before they finally reached the third floor. Each of the small nursery rooms was decorated with painted figures on the walls, though most of them were faded away. Some broken pieces of child-sized furniture stood in the corner along with a few torn children's books yellowed with age. Everything lay under a thick coat of dust.

The children spent the next couple hours sweeping, scrubbing, and gathering the odds and ends scattered about.

"It must have been so pretty when the Bugbee children lived here," Violet said as she swept some paper scraps into a dustbin. "Someone hand-painted all these clowns and animals on the walls. Now it's all going to be covered over. Let's save the different things we've found just in case the Bugbee children come back someday."

"Even if they did," Henry told Violet, "they'd be all grown up by now."

Jessie swept some cobwebs from the ceiling with a broom. "But guess what. Mabel told Grandfather that these will be kept as playrooms. When children come to visit their grandparents after House and Hands fixes up the house, they can play up here and in the playhouse."

"I hope so," Violet said. "Grandfather kept rooms for us at his house."

The children were quiet as they gathered up some items they had found. They searched around for Violet's music box with the dancing bear but didn't find it. As they quietly went about their work, the Aldens heard something. Footsteps!

"What's that?" Benny looked up. "Is

somebody walking on the roof? I hope that ceiling is good and strong."

Henry walked over to a window. "Ugh. These windows are hard to open. Oh, good, I got it. Anybody on the roof?" he yelled.

The footsteps stopped, but no one answered.

"That's weird," Henry said. "It sounds as if somebody was around here somewhere. But I don't see anyone." He banged the window down. "I'll go check the other rooms."

"Well, we're finished in here anyway." Jessie put away the cleaning supplies. "When Henry comes back, let's go downstairs."

"Nobody seems to be in the other rooms, either," Henry said when he returned. "I could have sworn someone was walking around up here."

With Henry leading the way, the children stepped into the hallway.

Henry saw a red-and-blue blur disappear down the stairs. "Hey!" he called out, before running ahead to the staircase. He looked down the winding banister all the way to the ground floor. "Brian! Wait up."

When Brian looked back up, five heads stared back.

The Aldens raced downstairs and caught up with Brian.

"You were rushing so fast," Henry said to Brian. "Were you working on the roof? We heard footsteps."

"No, I . . . uh . . . just came up to see how you were doing," Brian told the Aldens.

"But why did you rush off?" Henry asked. "If you were looking for us, I mean?"

Again, Brian's face got nearly as red as his shirt. "I . . . uh . . . heard my walkie-talkie. One of the volunteers needed me, that's all."

The Aldens thought this was odd, but none of them said anything until Soo Lee piped up. "There was a ghost on the roof walking around. My cousin Henry chased him away."

"It was probably some big blackbirds walking around up there," Brian said. "The roof tiles are kind of thin. You can hear birds and squirrels walking back and forth."

Jessie wasn't so sure. "These sounds were heavier than that. Is there another room near the nursery where somebody might be working?"

Now Brian really looked impatient with the Aldens. "You know, I really haven't got time to answer all these questions. Now that your work is finished up here, why don't you find the Gardiners? They must have some outdoor work that needs doing." With that, Brian pointed outside, where the Gardiners were carrying empty boxes into the garage.

"If you say so," Jessie told Brian before he went back upstairs.

"I feel as if Brian is always trying to get rid of us," Jessie said when the children stepped outside.

"Not just him — Nan and the Gardiners, too," Henry added. "They're always shooing us away. It seems like everyone is trying to keep us from poking around the house too much."

"Or from finding them poking around," Jessie added. "First the Gardiners didn't want us to help on the auction. Nan just disappears all the time. And Brian gets annoyed every time we find him here and there and everywhere. It's all very mysterious."

"I know," Henry said. "Let's go see if the Gardiners want us around or not."

The children met up with George and Louella outside the garage.

"Hi, George," Jessie said. "Brian thought you could use some help outside."

George stared at the children. "Not right now."

Louella pointed to the garden shed. "Well, I've got something for you children to do. Gather the branches your grandfather had the volunteers cut down. Then stack them near the shed. A tree company is sending over a wood chipper at the end of the week."

Soon the children were busy dragging heavy branches across the yard. As they worked, they noticed something curious going on.

Several times the Gardiners entered the garage with boxes and trash bags. Every now and then a car engine started up, then stopped.

"I overheard George telling Mabel that the two old cars in the garage won't start," Jessie whispered. "But it sounds as if someone is starting one of the cars."

"I know," Henry said. "Well, never mind the garage. Look who's on the third-floor landing — the window on the right. Isn't that Louella? Don't all stare at once."

The children took turns squinting at the window Henry was talking about.

"It sure looks like Louella!" Benny said in a loud whisper. "How'd she get there anyway?"

"Beats me," Henry answered. "I saw her go into the garage with George. I'm almost positive she never came out again."

"I wonder if there's a way to get to the

house from inside the garage," Jessie said.

"What are we waiting for?" Henry asked. "Let's see if she's still in there."

Jessie knocked on the garage door. "Louella? It's the Aldens. We finished the yard work you told us to do."

The children didn't hear any noise inside.

Jessie waited a few moments and called again. "Hello?"

Suddenly, they heard someone moving around even though the garage had sounded empty a moment ago.

"Who's there?" came Louella's voice, a little impatiently. It was as if she hadn't heard them before at all. "I'm coming."

Louella slowly opened the door.

The children looked at her, then quickly looked up at the house again. The person in the window was gone.

# CHAPTER 5

# Creaks and Squeaks

After dinner that night, nearly all the House and Hands volunteers had left for the day. The Aldens were in charge of doing the dinner dishes.

"That chocolate pudding was yummy," Benny said. He licked his spoon clean then dropped it into the soapy dishwater.

Mabel stuck her head in the kitchen door to say good night. "See you in the morning, children. I'm going off with the leaders to the building supply store. I'll drop them back here by nine tonight."

" 'Bye, Mabel," Jessie said. She sponged off the counter then poured out the dishpan. "Done. How about a game of checkers in the playhouse?" she asked the other children.

Henry had a different idea. "Instead of checkers, I'd like to check something else. We still haven't found Violet's missing music box. I don't know about you, but I keep wondering about all the other treasures that people thought belonged in the auction."

"A treasure hunt!" Benny said. "Let's go."

"Okay," Jessie agreed. "First let's stop by the playhouse for our jackets and flashlights."

"It's so dark, we need a flashlight to get to the flashlights," Henry joked as everyone stepped into the darkness.

The children crossed the lawn. Soo Lee and Benny jumped every time they stepped on the crackly branches and pinecones scattered in the yard.

"I'm glad you're staying in the playhouse

with us tonight," Jessie said, taking Soo Lee's hand. "Come see how nice it is — just like our boxcar."

She entered the playhouse first so she could turn on the camp lamp. The room filled with pretty yellow light. Violet had put up some old polka-dot curtains some-one had thrown out and hung them over the small windows. Everything was as cozy as could be.

"Okay, everybody have a flashlight?" Henry asked before turning off the camp light.

When the children returned to the main house, they were glad for their flashlights.

"I just remembered," Henry said. "Brian said there's only electricity on the first floor. Do you want to stay down here while I search upstairs?" he asked the other chil-dren. "I won't be gone long."

"We want to come!" Benny said. "We're not scared of the dark." But he stayed close to Henry all the same.

With Henry leading the way and Jessie at the back, the five Aldens climbed the creaky

steps. Their flashlights made shadows on the walls.

The children reached the second floor. They went up and down the hallway checking each door.

"Darn!" Henry said. "Most of the doors are locked. We won't get much treasure hunting done tonight. Maybe we ought to play that game of checkers after all."

"No way!" Benny said. He was feeling very brave and very curious. "Can we go to the garage? Grandfather said the two old cars in there are like the ones his family had when he was little."

"Yes," Jessie agreed. "I'd like to get in there. Maybe we can find a secret way from the garage to the house. It still seems strange that right after we saw Louella go into the garage we all thought we saw her in the house."

The garage was another old topsy-turvy building on the Bugbee estate. Everything about it was crooked — from the roof to the doors barely hanging on their hinges.

The doors creaked when Henry opened

them. He beamed his flashlight around inside. Seeing a lightbulb, he pulled a string to turn it on. It snapped right off in his hand! "I'll prop up a couple of flashlights so we can see what we're doing," he said.

"Uh-oh!" Benny said. "Now we can sort of see what the spiders are doing, too."

The children looked up at the garage ceiling. Huge cobwebs hung from every corner.

"Do you want to wait outside with Violet?" Jessie asked the younger children.

"I'm not scared of spiders," Soo Lee said, but she took Violet's hand.

With the other flashlights, the children checked every corner of the garage.

"I don't see any doorways or hatchways that lead to the house," Jessie said as she walked around the cars.

"There's no other way to get outside except through the doors we opened," Violet pointed out.

"Unless Louella climbed out that window," Henry said. He walked over to the only window in the garage. It was old and cracked. "This window is nailed shut with some rusty nails," Henry told the other children. "No one has opened it for a very long time. I give up."

"Can we look in these neat old cars?" Benny asked after his eyes got used to the dim light.

"Sure," Henry answered. "These cars are almost as old as Grandfather."

"I know," Violet said. "I saw a picture of Grandfather in a car like this. But it was clean and shiny."

"I wish we could make these cars clean and shiny, too," Jessie said, opening one of the car doors.

"Aaah!" the five children screamed all at once.

"A mouse!" Henry yelled. "There must be mice living in these cars. We've disturbed them."

Suddenly a huge spotlight shone in the children's faces. "And I've disturbed you snooping where you shouldn't be," a loud man's voice said.

The Aldens couldn't tell who was there.

Finally Jessie stepped away from the bright spotlight so she could get a better look. "Oh, Mr. Gardiner," she said. "We were just looking at these nice old cars. Our grandfather used to have a car like this one."

"That's all well and good," George Gardiner said in a growly voice. "But I'm sure Mr. Alden wouldn't have wanted a bunch of kids to be climbing over a valuable automobile like you are all doing now."

"Sorry," Henry said when he stepped away from the beam of George's huge flashlight. "We only opened the door to this old car. We didn't go inside. We were just thinking that we could help you clean these up when work on the house is finished. I bet these cars are worth a lot of money. If you move them out to the driveway, we could run a hose from the house to wash them."

This seemed to make George even more annoyed with the Aldens. "These cars haven't been driven in years."

This was too much for Benny. "But

Henry heard you and Mrs. Gardiner start one of the cars today. And we saw her —" Benny stopped when Jessie lightly stepped on his toe so he wouldn't say another word.

"There'll be no driving of these cars any-time soon," George said. "You kids have a playhouse. Now get yourselves there instead of snooping around where you don't be-long."

The Aldens trooped out of the garage.

Back in the playhouse, the children began talking all at once as they got ready for bed.

"I know we heard one of those cars start," Henry said. "But now George says the cars don't run."

"There's something about that garage that he doesn't want us to see," Jessie said. "Well, all we can do is keep a close eye on the Gardiners whenever they're in there."

"We'll sure need a lot of eyes," Henry added. "We've got to watch the Gardiners, plus Brian. He's always sending us away from the house, especially when we're up-stairs."

"Right," Jessie said. "And don't forget

Nan. Everyone's always looking for her because she's never where she's supposed to be."

Violet wondered about something, too. "Do you think all of them are working together somehow? I mean, trying to keep things secret from Mabel and the volunteers?"

By this time, the children were too tired after their busy day to come up with any answers.

"Is it time for bed?" Soo Lee asked.

Jessie answered by giving Soo Lee a big hug. "It sure is. Here's your warm, cozy sleeping bag. Let's tuck ourselves in and read the story of *The Little House*."

By the time the rest of the grown-ups returned to the big house later on, the Aldens were fast asleep in their own little house.

CHAPTER 6

## *Mysterious Music*

"My muscles are real strong now!" Benny said as he and the other Aldens climbed to the third floor of the Bugbee House the next day. Nan was following right behind, rushing as usual to get the Aldens working and out of her way.

After three days, the Aldens were used to climbing a lot of stairs.

"You go up and down these stairs even more than we do," Jessie said to Nan.

Nan paused on the second-floor landing.

"What do you mean? I work all over the house, not just up here."

Jessie looked at Nan for a few seconds. "It's . . . well, it's just that we run into you and Brian up here more than anybody else."

Nan disagreed. "I can't speak for Brian. But I'm sure you're quite mistaken about me. I'm hardly up here at all."

The Aldens didn't say anything else to Nan. Even after a few days, the children had a hard time figuring her out. She was a bit forgetful, always darting in and out of rooms and saying she left something behind. For someone who carried a notebook with her everywhere, she wasn't very organized.

"Now, where did Mabel say the bucket was?" Nan tried several doors before she finally found the right closet on the second floor. "Here it is. Just fill this bucket with water from the third-floor bathroom and use it to paste the wallpaper," she told the Aldens. "Some of the volunteers started papering the hallway up there, but they only finished a little of the job. Think you can do it?"

"We helped Uncle Joe wallpaper Soo Lee's bedroom," Jessie answered. "He taught us how to match up the paper and paste it up and everything."

"Fine," Nan said. "You'll find rolls of wallpaper, brushes, sponges, and a stepladder up there. The job will keep you busy most of today. Now I have work to do, and I don't want any interruptions. So long."

The Aldens got their water bucket and brought it to the third floor. They could hear Nan banging one door after the other on the second floor, directly below them.

The children looked at one another.

"It never seems like she's actually working," Jessie said. "She's always going off someplace with that notebook of hers."

Henry agreed. "I've yet to see her pick up a broom or a tool, that's for sure."

"Here's another strange thing," Violet said when she came out of the bathroom with the bucket of water. "This hallway is already wallpapered. See? Somebody did most of the job already. I wonder why Nan told us it would take us all day to finish. I don't even think she checked."

Jessie walked to the far end of the hall. "Well, there's still one roll that needs to be put up at this end. I guess we should get started."

After the children lined up their equipment, Henry found a stepladder and climbed up. He measured the ceiling to the floor. "Cut ninety-two inches," he told Violet and Jessie. "Remember what Uncle Joe said?"

The girls answered together. " 'Measure twice, cut once.' "

Soo Lee and Benny looked confused.

As Violet measured the wallpaper a second time, she explained what Uncle Joe meant. "If you measure something twice before cutting it, then you probably won't make a mistake and have to cut more than once. It could be wallpaper or a piece of wood or —"

"A piece of cake!" Benny said.

The children helped one another measure, cut, and paste a wallpaper strip.

"Ready, Henry?" Jessie called out.

"Ready!" Henry answered.

The other children carefully carried the wet wallpaper strip over to Henry. He lined it up, matching the leaf pattern exactly right. Then he smoothed the paper in place. There wasn't a bubble or a wrinkle on it. "Good job, everybody."

The children stepped back from the nice smooth wall to admire their work. That's when they heard someone walking around overhead.

"There are those footsteps again." Jessie scooted in the direction of the steps. But she couldn't see anyone. "It can't be Nan. She's downstairs."

"Maybe it's another mouse," Benny joked when Jessie came back puzzled.

"A mouse that plays music?" Soo Lee asked.

A faint, tinkling sound seemed to be coming from somewhere not too far away. The Aldens checked in all the third-floor rooms, but didn't get any closer to the music.

"It's 'The Teddy Bears' Picnic'!" Violet said. "Listen."

"Maybe the sound is somehow coming from the second floor where Nan is," Henry whispered. "I'll go check."

He tiptoed down one flight of stairs but didn't hear a thing. One room was locked. Raising his hand, Henry knocked on the door.

"Who's there?" Nan yelled out, but she didn't open the door.

"It's Henry. Can I come in?"

"No, I'm painting in here," Nan snapped. "All the woodwork is wet with paint. Go finish your wallpapering."

Henry started to say something but stopped himself. "Okay."

When he got back to the other children, he explained what had happened. "You know what? I didn't smell a bit of paint coming from that room. I wonder why Nan locked herself in there."

Violet looked at Henry with her big blue eyes. "Did you hear my music box?"

Henry shook his head. "I'm not sure

where that sound came from. I didn't hear it from where Nan was, anyway. But she may have heard my footsteps and closed the music box."

"What are we going to do now?" Violet asked.

"I guess we'll clean up, then go downstairs to see if there are other jobs for us," Jessie answered.

"Can I climb up on there?" Benny asked when he saw Henry about to fold the stepladder. "I want to be tall."

Henry smiled. "Sure. We need to be careful around ladders. So lean against the wall with your right hand. I'll hold you and the ladder steady."

"Now I'm taller than you!" Benny said when he stood on top of the stepladder. He looked up at the ceiling and noticed something. "Know what? There's a little knob on the ceiling that sticks out."

Henry held his arms out for Benny. "Here, jump down. I want to get a closer look. Jessie, hold the stepladder steady for me, okay?"

Jessie held the ladder firmly as Henry stood on top.

"Good eyes, Benny," Henry said when he saw something on the ceiling, too. "From down there you can't really see that knob. I wonder if it's part of a folding staircase like Aunt Jane had at her ranch house. I can't quite reach it."

Jessie squinted up. "Oh, I see what you're talking about. The knob blends into the carvings on the ceiling."

The knob was just a couple of inches out of Henry's reach. "Know what?" he said. "I'm going to stand on the floor instead. If I put Soo Lee on my shoulders, she can pull the panel open a couples of inches. Then I can pull it down the rest of the way."

Soo Lee always loved sitting on Henry's shoulders. She was even more excited now to help her cousins open the secret door. She looked down at the other children after Henry put her on his shoulders. "Now I'm tall, too!"

"Okay, Soo Lee, just tug that knob a teeny bit," Jessie said, looking up.

A moment later, the children were startled when a figure appeared in the hallway.

"May I ask what you children are doing?" Louella Gardiner demanded in a sharp voice. "Why is that child sitting on your shoulders?"

Henry reached up for Soo Lee and helped her down.

Soo Lee came to the rescue. "We were listening to see if there was a mouse on the roof."

"A mouse? On the roof?" Louella said. "This is exactly why I told Mabel Hart that children should not be volunteers. Now I'd like you all to go work outside with my husband. There's still a lot of yard work to be done. You'll do less damage out there than inside."

"But we finished wallpapering," Henry began, "like Nan told us to."

Now Louella looked even more annoyed. "That one! A more scatterbrained leader I've never seen than Nan Lodge — always with her nose in a book or scribbling down jobs to do instead of doing them. Why, I told her the wallpapering job was nearly complete yesterday. And it certainly wasn't a job for children. Now go find Mr. Gardiner outside."

After the children went downstairs, something kept bothering Jessie. "Did any of you see or hear Louella come up the stairs? Didn't it seem as if she just appeared out of nowhere on the third floor?"

"I know," Henry agreed. "I just hope she doesn't look up and notice that secret panel in the ceiling."

"Unless she already knows about it," Jessie added.

CHAPTER 7

# A Crash in the Dark

Late that night, in the middle of the night, the little playhouse where the Aldens were camped out shook in the wind.

Jessie reached over and tapped Henry's shoulder. "Henry, are you awake?"

"I'm glad you're up, Jessie," Henry whispered back. "I hope all this wind and rain doesn't wake up the others. And that the roof on the playhouse doesn't leak, either."

Just as Henry sat up, he and Jessie heard a huge boom outside.

All at once, the younger children woke up, too.

"What was that big crash?" Soo Lee asked. She snuggled close to Jessie's sleeping bag.

"There, there, Soo Lee," Jessie said. "It's a storm. Henry is going to check on what that noise was."

Henry grabbed his flashlight and stepped outside. As soon as he opened the playhouse door, the rain and wind slapped against him. He beamed his flashlight across the property. A huge tree branch had crashed to the ground just a few feet from the playhouse. Then he saw another beam of light cross with his. "Who's out there?" he yelled, but the wind carried his words away.

The flashlight grew closer. Brian was holding it. "Gather up the other kids to bring them to the main house," Brian told Henry. "We're asking all the volunteers camping on the property to move indoors. Bring your sleeping bags and whatever else you need — especially flashlights. We've lost all electricity and heat in the house."

With that, Brian disappeared into the rain and darkness.

Henry stepped back inside the playhouse. He left his flashlight on. "Okay, everybody. Brian just told us that everyone who's camping out has to go to the main house during the storm. Get your flashlights and jackets. Jessie and I will help you roll up your sleeping bags."

A few minutes later, the wind and rain died down a bit. "Okay," Jessie said. "There's a break in the storm. Let's make a run for it to the main house. Ready, everybody?"

"Ready!" Benny said. He was excited to be up in the middle of the night, even if things were crashing around them. "It's okay, Soo Lee. You can hold Jessie's hand. And I'll hold Henry's hand."

Jessie grabbed the camp light and led everyone out.

"Wow, what a huge tree branch!" Henry said when the children stepped over it. "We were lucky it wasn't any bigger. It sure left a big empty spot up there. Hey, look!" he

said, pointing up. "Did you notice that skylight before — there, up on the roof near the nursery wing? See?"

Jessie looked up, even though all she wanted to do was get inside where it was warm and dry. "I don't remember seeing any room with a skylight in that part of the house before. I guess the tree branch that fell hid it from view. There's a light moving around in there, too — like somebody's flashlight. Let's go inside."

When the Aldens finally stepped into the Bugbee House, it was pretty dark and buzzing with people. Several volunteers beamed their flashlights at the children when they came inside.

"Hey, Aldens!" one of the volunteers said after he recognized the children. "That was a pretty scary noise!"

"We weren't scared," Benny answered. "Well, maybe just a little bit."

Mabel arrived just then and came over to the Aldens.

"You are very brave children," she said. "Nan told me there was quite a crash when that tree limb came down. She called me immediately. I told her to round up everyone who was camping on the property. I'm glad she got you in here so quickly."

The Aldens were puzzled.

"Brian was the one who came over and told us to come into the main house," Jessie told Mabel. "Not Nan."

Mabel looked puzzled and a little annoyed. "Oh, dear. I must say, Nan and I are always crossing messages. Well, never mind. The most important thing is that you children are out of harm's way." Mabel put one arm around Soo Lee and the other around Benny. "The second most important thing is that this house is out of harm's way, too. At least I think so. I expect Brian and the Gardiners are checking the house to make sure we didn't lose any windows or roof shingles."

"Or skylights," Jessie whispered to Henry.

"The heat just went off," Mabel continued. "But since warm air rises, it will stay toastier for a while on the upper floor. So why don't you go find an empty room upstairs to sleep in? The third floor has a working bathroom, so try there first. Would you mind that?"

"Not a bit," Jessie said.

"Good," Mabel said. "Now I wonder where my leaders have gone off to. I must say, I'm not quite as alert in the middle of the night. If you see the Gardiners or Nan or Brian around, tell them to find me."

"Sure thing," Jessie told Mabel. "See you in the morning."

"This *is* the morning," Benny said. "But the dark part."

The children carried their sleeping bags all the way to the third floor.

"It's a lucky thing Mabel sent us up here," Henry said in a whisper. "She said we can find a room. While we're up here, maybe we can figure out where that skylight room is."

"And who was in it," Jessie said. "Don't forget that."

But when the children checked the doors on the third floor, they discovered all of them locked except for the bathroom.

"Let's try the second floor." Henry walked back down a flight of stairs. "There's one room unlocked down here," he called up to the other children. "Come on down."

The unlocked room was small and snug — just big enough for the children's sleeping bags. In no time, they arranged their bags on the floor.

The sleeping bags were ready for sleeping, but the Aldens weren't.

"I'm not tired," Benny announced. His blue eyes were as wide as if it were the middle of the day, not the middle of the night.

"We should try to get some sleep," Jessie said. "We need our rest so we can work hard tomorrow." Jessie turned off the camp light.

"Hey, someone's in the hallway," Benny whispered a few minutes later.

The door opened, and a light shone in. The children couldn't see who was there. They pretended to be asleep.

"Did you see who that was, Henry?" Benny asked.

"No," Henry said, "but the footsteps are going away. Whoever it was is gone."

The Aldens always enjoyed whispering to one another before falling asleep — especially in strange new places.

"I wish we could go see where those secret stairs in the ceiling go to," Benny said in the dark.

Jessie wriggled in her sleeping bag. "I was just thinking the same thing. I suppose we could take a peek now that everyone else is asleep downstairs. Maybe those stairs lead to the room that has the skylight."

One by one the Aldens slipped out of their sleeping bags and into the hallway.

Soo Lee was in her bare feet. "This floor is wet," she said when she came out of the room.

Jessie bent down to touch the floor. She slipped out of her shoes so she could feel the floor. "Let's follow these wet spots," Jessie whispered. "Somebody must have come up here from the outside. If we follow these footprints, maybe we can figure out where the person went."

"Good thinking," Henry said to Jessie. "Lead the way."

Jessie and Soo Lee tracked the wet footprints to the third-floor hallway.

When the footprints stopped, so did the Aldens. They found themselves directly under the ceiling panel they had discovered the morning before.

Henry aimed his flashlight upward. "Who wants a boost up on my shoulders?" Henry whispered. "I need Soo Lee or Benny to tug the knob."

Before Benny or Soo Lee could decide, the children heard a creak coming from the ceiling. The panel started to open right where the Aldens were standing!

Jessie motioned to the nearby bathroom and opened the door. The other children squeezed in behind her. They climbed into the claw-footed tub and hid themselves behind an old shower curtain. Jessie put her finger up to her lips so no one would speak.

A couple of minutes later, the children

heard a springy sound, followed by a faint thud, then another springy sound. Some footsteps came close to the bathroom where the children were hiding. The door opened. A dim light swept over the bathroom.

The Aldens could barely breathe. What if the person found them huddled behind the shower curtain? The children stood as still as statues. Eventually they heard footsteps going downstairs. They waited in the tub for several minutes. Finally they felt safe enough to climb out.

"I think whoever that was is gone now," Henry whispered. He stuck his head out and checked the dark hallway. "Which way, guys? Follow the person down the regular staircase or go up the disappearing staircase?"

The other children looked at one another.

"We might not get another chance to go up there alone," Jessie pointed out.

Violet looked up at the staircase panel in the ceiling. "Maybe my music box is up there."

"And who knows what else we might find?" Henry said. "After we get a look around, we can keep a watch out for anyone else we find up here."

"Let's go," Benny said, following the beam of Henry's flashlight down the dark hall.

# CHAPTER 8

# The Disappearing Staircase Appears

The Aldens tiptoed into the hallway behind Henry. They stood under the secret ceiling panel.

Jessie beamed her flashlight upward. "Hey, look. Whoever was up here didn't close the panel all the way. It's hanging open partway. I think we can reach it from the stepladder. Bring it over."

Jessie was right. Even though she was two inches shorter than Henry, she easily reached the knob from the top of the stepladder. The panel made a springy sound and came down a couple of feet. "All I have to do is unfold the steps the rest of the way," Jessie said, doing just that.

Henry caught the steps before they landed on the floor. He didn't want to make any extra noise.

The disappearing staircase filled the hallway. The Aldens got in line, eager to go up.

"I'll stay down here to keep a lookout in case that person comes back," Henry said. "We could solve two mysteries at the same time — finding some missing treasures and whoever knows about them. Good luck."

As Henry stood by, the other children carefully climbed the wooden steps.

"I hope this attic is filled with treasures," Violet whispered when she reached the top step.

Violet wasn't disappointed. "There's another playroom above the nursery! Only smaller," she said in a whisper.

The children flashed their flashlights around the room. The child-sized space had low ceilings and shelves. Everywhere their flashlight beams landed, the children saw

toys — heaps of them. Beautiful old dolls and stuffed animals stared back at the Aldens from the shelves. Toy trucks, wagons, old-fashioned roller skates, and even a train track filled another side of the room.

"Wow, that train set is huge!" Benny said in a loud whisper. "Too bad the electricity isn't on to make all those train cars go around."

Jessie opened the doors of a cabinet. "Look! More old trucks — lots of them," she said.

Violet and Soo Lee went over to a large dollhouse displayed on its own special table.

"It's a miniature model of the Bugbee House," Violet said in her soft voice, "only the way it must have looked when the Bugbee children lived here. It even has a secret playroom just like the one we're standing in."

The Aldens gathered around the dollhouse. It was completely furnished right down to many of the very toys the children could see in the actual playroom. For a few seconds, no one spoke. The dollhouse, all furnished and complete with a family of little plastic people, looked like such a happy place. To the Aldens, the real Bugbee House now seemed empty and sad.

Jessie noticed something else about the dollhouse. "Look. There's a tiny skylight just like the one we saw where the tree branch fell down."

The children looked up at the playroom ceiling.

"But there's no skylight in here," Violet said. "In the dollhouse, the skylight is in a different space — in a room that's behind the third-floor bathroom."

"You're right, Violet," Jessie said. "But I didn't notice any other entrances in the bathroom before. We'd better go back and check."

"Oh, dear, one other thing." Violet pointed to something else in the dollhouse. "Look, there's a miniature music box in the dollhouse playroom with a tiny bear on it! Maybe that means . . ." She turned around to face the actual shelf in the actual playroom.

"My music box!" she said in an excited whisper. She picked it up. "It's the very one I bid on. There's even a price sticker on it."

"Then take it," said Jessie. "We'll tell Mabel we found it after all, then you can pay for it. We have to let her know about this room and all these valuable old toys. Whoever was up here is keeping it a secret, so it's up to us to tell her."

Violet picked up the music box with the dancing bear. "I won't play it right now. Someone might hear the music just like we did. I wonder who was up here."

"That's what we need to find out."

The children took one last look around the hidden playroom. Then, one by one, they climbed down the disappearing staircase to the bottom, where Henry was still keeping a lookout.

"Okay," he said after everyone was back down in the hallway again. "Let's push these stairs back up into the ceiling. Benny and Soo Lee, you two be my lookouts in case anyone comes up here." Henry folded the steps, then gave the panel a firm push.

"Abracadabra. Staircase, disappear." And so it did!

"Violet has something special to show you," Jessie whispered to Henry.

"The attic up there is really a secret playroom full of old toys," Violet explained to Henry. "Somebody hid my music box there."

"Wow!" Henry said. "So it was stolen."

"Just like I said," Benny cried, excited about that idea.

The children examined the music box but didn't play it. They weren't taking any chances.

"It must be valuable," Jessie said. "Otherwise, why did someone go to all the bother of hiding it up in the hidden playroom?"

"What I wonder is, who knows about that playroom?" Henry asked.

"A person with big, wet feet," Soo Lee answered.

The children tried not to laugh too hard.

"That could be a lot of people in this house tonight. If I get a chance, I'd like to go up there and look around another time," Henry said. "Well, at least we figured out where the skylight is."

Jessie smacked her forehead. "Wait! We were so excited about finding Violet's music box, we almost forgot to tell you: The skylight isn't in the playroom at all. We think there's a hidden space behind the bathroom."

Henry couldn't get over this. "Wow! Well, I guess you're too tired to go looking around for it, right, guys?" he asked Soo Lee and Benny.

"I'm not too tired," Benny whispered right back.

Henry laughed. "Just kidding. Let's go."

By now the Aldens knew where all the squeaky parts of the floor were. They reached the bathroom without so much as a creak.

"There's the linen closet," Jessie said. "I don't see any openings or anything in here, though."

"Maybe the secret room was blocked off

a long time ago." Henry pushed hard on the wall behind the shelves. Nothing budged. "Hey, Soo Lee, what are you doing?"

Soo Lee, the shortest Alden, saw something the other children had missed. Looking straight ahead, she pointed below the shelf right at her eye level. "Look, Henry. There's a little door under this shelf. You have to be little like me and Benny to see it."

Henry crouched down. "Good job, Soo Lee." He lifted the two bottom shelves. "They aren't attached. Now we can get through that door easier, even though it's only about three feet tall. Ready?"

By this time, Benny planted himself right by Soo Lee. "Can I look — I mean, after Soo Lee gets her turn?"

Soo Lee backed away. "You can go first, Benny. Then me."

Benny had to stoop down a little to open the door. He pushed it gently just a crack.

"What do you see?" Henry asked.

"There's a room full of boxes and stuff,"

he said. "And it's got a skylight, just like in the dollhouse. Uh-oh." He backed out suddenly.

Benny put his finger to his lips. "Shhh." He pulled the door gently to close it. He pointed to the bathroom door.

The Aldens went into the hallway where they could talk.

"What did you see?" Jessie whispered. "Did someone come?"

"Mr. Gardiner! He's in there," Benny whispered. "He was putting things into cardboard boxes, but I couldn't tell what."

"One thing we need to find out," Henry said, "is how George got into that room. Did you notice an exit in the dollhouse room?"

Jessie shook her head no. Then she had a thought. "Maybe the passageway came later — after someone built the dollhouse."

"There's another way to get into that room, and it has something to do with the garage," Henry said. "We just haven't figured it out yet."

CHAPTER 9

# Lost and Found

The next day, the Aldens spent the morning painting the porch of the main house. While they worked, they spoke in low whispers.

"It's too bad Mabel is at the fund-raising breakfast right now," Jessie said. "We have to tell her about the disappearing staircase and the hidden playroom."

Violet touched up a spot Benny had missed on one of the railings. "I want to show her the music box."

"I want to go exploring," Benny said now that their work was all done.

"Painting these railings took longer than I expected," Henry said. "I don't think we have enough time to go exploring. Nan invited some television people to film us working, and they're supposed to be here any minute."

Jessie cleaned off the rim of the paint can, then hammered down the lid. "You know, we could give those reporters a real story and show them the staircase and secret rooms we found."

"Hey, that's a great idea," Henry said. "Everybody will be gathered around for that. Then we'd see who gets upset about the disappearing staircase."

"We might get to be on television," Benny told Soo Lee as Violet cleaned off their hands with a cloth. "Maybe the camera will follow us around. We can be famous!"

Jessie chuckled. "You're pretty famous already, Benny Alden! Well, let's go find the

Gardiners. I want to let them know we finished the painting job Nan asked us to do."

"The Gardiners are going out," Henry said. "See? They're heading to their van with some boxes. Brian, too."

Benny couldn't believe it. "Hey," he called out. "Don't you want to be famous? The TV people are here!"

Minutes later, the lawn in front of the Bugbee House was covered with cables, lights, and strange equipment.

"Can you show us around a little?" one television crew person asked the Aldens.

The Aldens immediately forgot about Brian and the Gardiners. The television people needed their help.

Soon a reporter was on the lawn talking into a camera about the House and Hands project. Then he introduced Mabel, who had just arrived.

"He's going over to interview Grandfather," Violet whispered a few minutes later.

The children went over to watch. Grandfather was explaining to the reporter how he'd discovered some prize rosebushes hidden under some vines.

The reporter spotted Benny off to the side. He came over with the camera operator.

"Well, young man, your grandfather told us you've been working on the Bugbee House, too. He found some old rosebushes nobody knew were there. Did you and the other children find anything?"

"A big staircase that disappears into a ceiling," Benny blurted out, to everyone's amazement. "Nobody knows about it. Well, maybe somebody. We heard footsteps walking around! And a person even came down the steps. Wanna see?"

The reporter seemed eager to follow Benny into the house. "Let's turn off the cameras for now until we find out what this boy is talking about."

Benny led a parade of visitors and volunteers up to the third floor. The other children followed right behind.

Benny pointed to the ceiling on the third floor. "The staircase is up there. It folds out. It's hard to see 'cause somebody hid it. But we found it! I have to get up on my brother Henry's shoulders to pull the steps down."

"Well, go right ahead," said the reporter.

Henry boosted Benny up. He pulled at the knob.

"Stand back, everybody," Henry said.

Everyone gasped when Henry swung the staircase down.

"Why, I'll be," Mabel said. "I thought I knew this house inside out. I misplaced the blueprints before I had a chance to study them."

"There's a whole big playroom up there where kids used to play," Benny told everyone. "We can go up."

The reporter chuckled. "Lead the way, Aldens," he said, following the children up the staircase.

Benny stopped suddenly on the top step. "Brian! How'd you get here? This room's a big secret."

"What's going on, Brian?" Jessie asked when she and everyone else climbed into

the attic. "We thought you left with the Gardiners."

Brian looked around at all the faces waiting for an explanation. "I don't know where the Gardiners are. I went out to my truck to get something. I came back to measure some . . ." He stopped when his eyes fell on Mabel's upset face.

"But Brian," Mabel said after looking around at all the hidden treasures. "You knew about this attic? Why didn't you tell me? Why, these wonderful old toys could have been put up for auction to help out our group. Were you planning to keep these valuable things hidden?"

Now it was Brian's turn to look upset. He could hardly look at Mabel. "I did plan to tell you before we finished work on the house so that you could have another auction. I wasn't going to keep anything except . . ."

"How did you even know about this room?" Mabel asked.

Brian looked around. Everyone's eyes were fixed on him. "From my mother," he answered. "She was Mr. Bugbee's daughter. Mr. Bugbee was my grandfather, though I never knew him. My mother grew up in this house until she was eight years old. My grandparents had to sell his business, this house, and everything in it to pay the taxes he'd forgotten about. He didn't steal anything, though — just plain forgot. But by the time he paid the tax bill, he couldn't face the townspeople and their stories anymore. He took what little money he had left and moved his whole family far away. Afterward, a lot of bad stories about the family started going around. I heard them all when I moved back."

Mabel moved toward Brian. She put her hand on his arm. "Even if these objects once belonged to your family, they weren't yours to take, Brian," she said gently. "They belonged to the person who bought the house. Then he left everything to House and Hands. All this belongs to our group."

Brian looked at Mabel. "I know. I hope you'll believe I wasn't going to take anything. I wanted some time alone to look around up here by myself — to find out more about my family. They're all gone now except for me. I wasn't going to take any of it, not even the music box. I tried to bid on it, but I was too late. My mother told me it was the only thing she wished she still had."

The room was still. "I've always wanted to come back here," Brian said in a soft voice. "It was only a coincidence that I found out the house was being fixed up. A roofer who works for me volunteers for other House and Hands projects around the country. He mentioned it."

Everyone stayed silent, sad for the young man.

Finally Violet stepped forward. "I found the music box up here the other day. I was going to pay the Gardiners for it before we left. I'll give it to you, Brian."

"Thanks, Violet," Brian said. "Don't worry. I'll pay for it." He looked straight at the reporter. "I don't want to add another bad story to the Bugbee name."

The reporter looked even more confused

than everyone else did. He turned to Nan. "Is this why you really called us here?" he asked. "To expose the theft of a music box?"

Nan didn't say anything. She looked straight at Brian. "I can't believe you're related to the Bugbees, too."

Now it was Brian's turn to be surprised. "What?"

"My grandmother was Mr. Bugbee's sister," Nan blurted out. "Unfortunately, Grandma died before she could clear my great-uncle's name. My dad said Grandma always wanted to put an end to all the rumors that her brother left town without paying his tax debts. At first she believed the rumors, too. They stopped speaking to each other after that. Our families never met again."

"Until now," Mabel pointed out. "You two are second cousins, and you didn't even know it. What I don't understand is why you came here, Nan. Just curiosity?"

"More than curiosity," Nan began. "My father told me that after the fire in the Greenfield Town Hall, the tax records were lost. He said there were probably old records in the house that would prove Mr. Bugbee was free and clear of debt when he left Greenfield. I've been following news about this house for some time. That's how I found out that you needed volunteers for House and Hands. I signed up to work on it — and look around for proof that my great-uncle paid all his debts. That's why I called the television station here — and to help us raise money, too."

By this time Grandfather Alden had joined everyone in the attic playroom, too. "Is that why you wanted to look through my bound copies of old Greenfield newspapers in my den? I'm sorry to say that Mr. Bugbee's name never was cleared as far as anyone knows. It didn't help that he kept to himself — then just up and left with his family like he had something to be ashamed of."

That's when Nan stepped forward to show Mr. Alden some papers in her notebook. "Here's what I came to find," Nan said. "I discovered these paid tax receipts in an old cardboard box. I'm sorry I didn't get much work done, Mabel. Whenever I could take a few minutes away from working on the house, I went hunting for anything that would prove my great-uncle wasn't some kind of thief."

"There, there," Mabel said. "Your work was important, too — clearing the Bugbee name. Thank goodness for the Aldens and the rest of the volunteers. They pitched in to help you and Brian and the Gardiners. And they led us to all these treasures. Not to mention all their hard work."

"It's okay to mention it," Benny said.

Everyone in the playroom chuckled.

Mabel looked around the room. "I wonder what Louella and George will think of all this. Where are the Gardiners, anyway?"

But there was no answer. The Gardiners had disappeared.

# CHAPTER 10

# No Escape

The reporter stood off in the corner of the playroom and looked a little restless. "I guess we have our story, Nan. I'll run a little piece about your great-uncle and about House and Hands fixing up the Bugaboo House."

"Please don't call it that," Nan protested. "My great-uncle was a bit odd but not scary. He made this whole place into a playhouse for his family. He designed it with all kinds of hallways, secret closets, doors that don't go anywhere, windows that open to other rooms instead of outside. But it wasn't a scary house."

"Fine," the reporter said. "Well, show us around. I suppose we can get some shots of the house's oddities."

Benny stepped in front of Nan. "Know what? We found another secret room filled with old stuff. And know what else? George knows where it is, too."

The reporter nodded to the camera operator. "Let's follow this boy. Where to now, young man?"

"To the bathroom on the third floor," Benny answered.

"The bathroom?" Mabel asked, a bit confused.

"Don't worry, Mabel," Jessie said. "Wait until you see what Benny and Soo Lee found."

By this time, both children had gone down the staircase. By the time everyone had joined them, Benny and Soo Lee had already exposed the hidden door in the bathroom.

"See?" Benny said to the reporter. "This

doorway goes to another room. Isn't it neat?"

The reporter bent down to get a better look. "Are you sure this opens? It won't budge."

Henry came over. "Let me try." He gave the hidden door a strong push with his feet.

Everyone heard a thud on the other side.

"It's open!" Henry bent down and entered the hidden room. "George! Louella! So you didn't leave." He looked around at the heaps of old leather books, jewelry boxes, and paintings all boxed up and ready to go. "So this is where you kept all the treasures that never got into the auction. Well, now they will."

George grabbed a box and ran out a door on the far side of the room. Louella quickly disappeared behind her husband. The door banged shut behind them with a click.

Henry pulled at the door. "It's locked!"

Benny scooted over and put his ear up against the door. "Now I remember something. When Soo Lee and I got lost, we heard people walking and talking behind the walls and some steps, too. I forgot."

Jessie nodded. "Yes. Well, we had a feeling the Gardiners knew there were more treasures in this house."

"I have a hunch the passageway they used goes right to the garage," Henry said. "Follow us."

The Aldens scrambled out of the hidden room as fast as they could get through the opening. In a flash, they raced down several flights of stairs and out to the garage.

The Gardiners were already backing one of the old cars down the driveway.

"Stop!" Henry yelled.

Jessie spotted a big lawn mower. She raced over and pushed it into the driveway. This blocked the car from going any farther.

George turned off the engine then banged his fist on the steering wheel. He and Louella stared straight ahead. The Aldens had them trapped.

By this time, everyone else had come outside, too.

The reporter raced over and looked in the car window. "That's the pair that made off with half the contents of the Paulding estate over in Winslow last month," he said. "These two have quite a racket going. They show up at big estates that are about to be sold. They work there for a while and pass themselves off as auction experts — which they are. That's how they know which stuff to steal before it ever gets to auction. They sneak out the real treasures and leave the rest for the auction." He turned to Mabel. "I bet you everything they took is worth ten times more than what you made at the auction."

Mabel swallowed hard and tapped her fingers against the old car. "It's all my fault. I hired them."

"So did a lot of smart people, Mrs. Hart," the reporter said. "You're not the first. But thanks to the Aldens, this is the first time they've been caught red-handed."

"Oh, my," Mabel said when she spotted some rolled-up papers in the backseat. "Those are the house blueprints I thought

I lost. So that's how they figured out where the roomful of treasures was. But the Gardiners didn't count on the Aldens. These kids didn't need blueprints to find the hidden rooms."

Brian turned to Mabel. "Well," he said, "now we can plan another auction."

"Another auction?" Mabel said. "It's hard to think about that right now. We'd better get the police here."

"I'm making the call right now," the reporter said, holding up his cell phone. "These two aren't going anywhere."

"Yes, they are," Henry said. "While we're waiting, I want them to show us how they got from the garage to the house. We knew there was a way, but George sent us out of there before we could find it." He opened the car door for Louella.

Louella unlocked the garage door. Everyone followed her inside.

"A trapdoor!" Benny cried when he spotted a wooden door on the garage floor. "It was under the car."

"So that's why we kept hearing a car engine sometimes when the Gardiners were in the garage," Henry said. He went over and pulled up the door. "There are some steps."

"Can I look?" Benny said.

The Aldens climbed down some wooden steps to a basement under the garage. They didn't have their flashlights, but there was enough light to see something up ahead.

"It's a spiral staircase," Jessie said when she went over. "It goes way, way up to the third floor."

A few people crowded around to get a look.

Brian smacked his forehead. "Now I remember this passageway," Brian said. "My dad mentioned that my grandfather had a chauffeur named Wolcott. He lived in a small room on the third floor near the bathroom. He complained all the time about how much he disliked going outside in bad weather to start the car. My grandfather put this staircase in an airshaft so Wolcott could go right to the garage from the bathroom. Of course, as a joke, he made it tricky for Wolcott to get to the passageway. The bathroom doorway is just a few feet high, whereas Wolcott was a very tall man. Well, what do you know?"

"I know something," Benny said as everyone walked outside again.

"What's that?" Grandfather asked, wondering what Benny was up to next.

"I'm hungry," Benny said. "That's what I know. Didn't somebody say there was going to be a picnic after the television people left?"

Mabel came over and hugged Benny. "After we settle things with the police, we'll have our picnic and plan a new auction."

"Know what kind of picnic?" Benny asked the crowd.

Everyone quieted down to hear what Benny was going to say next.

"A teddy bear picnic!" Benny announced.

# THE BOXCAR CHILDREN

## Fan Club

## Join the Boxcar Fan Club!

Visit **boxcarchildren.com** and receive a free goodie
bag when you sign up. You'll receive occasional
newsletters and be eligible to win prizes
and more! Sign up today!

## Don't Forget!

The Boxcar Children audiobooks are also available!
Find them at your local bookstore, or visit
**oasisaudio.com** for more information.

BASED ON THE **WORLDWIDE BEST-SELLI**

ZACHARY
**GORDON**

JOEY
**KING**

MACKENZIE
**FOY**

JADON
**SAND**

THE

# BOXCAR
## CHILDREN

WITH
**J.K. SIMMONS**

AND
**MARTIN SHEEN**

"a warm and wonderful film that the entire family can enjoy
THE DOVE FOUNDATION

# NOW AVAILABLE!
### THE BOXCAR CHILDREN DVD!

## The first full-length animated feature based on Gertrude Chandler Warner's beloved children's novel!

Featuring an all-star cast of voice actors including Academy Award–winner J. K. Simmons (*Whiplash*), Academy Award–nominee Martin Sheen (*Apocalypse Now*), and Zachary Gordon (*Diary of a Wimpy Kid*), Joey King (*Fargo*), Mackenzie Foy (*The Twilight Saga: Breaking Dawn*), and Jadon Sand (*The LEGO Movie*)

## Available for sale or download wherever DVDs are sold

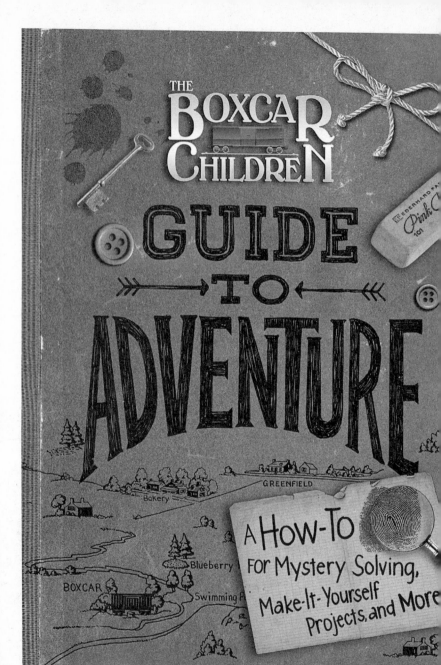

# THE BOXCAR CHILDREN

# GUIDE
>»—TO—«
# ADVENTURE

GREENFIELD

Bakery

Blueberry

BOXCAR

Swimming P

A How-To
For Mystery Solving,
Make-It-Yourself
Projects, and More

ISBN: 9780807509050, $12

# Create everyday adventures with the *Boxcar Children Guide to Adventure!*

A fun compendium filled with tips and tricks from the Boxcar Children—from making invisible ink and secret disguises, creating secret codes, and packing a suitcase to taking the perfect photo and enjoying the great outdoors.

# Available wherever books are sold

GERTRUDE CHANDLER WARNER discovered when she was teaching that many readers who like an exciting story could find no books that were both easy and fun to read. She decided to try to meet this need, and her first book, *The Boxcar Children*, quickly proved she had succeeded.

Miss Warner drew on her own experiences to write the mystery. As a child she spent hours watching trains go by on the tracks opposite her family home. She often dreamed about what it would be like to set up housekeeping in a caboose or freight car—the situation the Alden children find themselves in.

While the mystery element is central to each of Miss Warner's books, she never thought of them as strictly juvenile mysteries. She liked to stress the Aldens' independence and resourcefulness and their solid New England devotion to using up and making do. The Aldens go about most of their adventures with as little adult supervision as possible—something else that delights young readers.

Miss Warner lived in Putnam, Connecticut, until her death in 1979. During her lifetime, she received hundreds of letters from girls and boys telling her how much they liked her books.